CREEPY CREATURES

TOAD TERROR

Collect all the
CREEPY CREATURES

SNAKE SHOCK

SPIDER FRIGHT

BAT ATTACK

RAT PANIC

TOAD TERROR

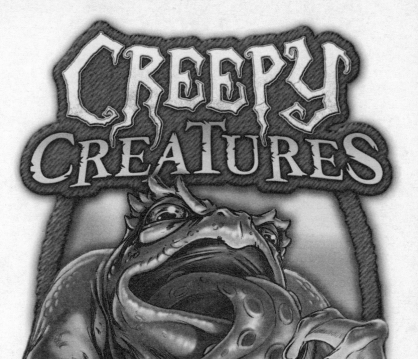

CREEPY CREATURES

TOAD TERROR

ED GRAVES

■SCHOLASTIC

First published in the UK in 2011 by Scholastic Children's Books
An imprint of Scholastic Ltd
Euston House, 24 Eversholt Street
London, NW1 1DB, UK
Registered office: Westfield Road, Southam,
Warwickshire, CV47 0RA
SCHOLASTIC and associated logos are trademarks
and/or registered trademarks of Scholastic Inc.
Series created by Working Partners Ltd

Text copyright © Working Partners, 2011

ISBN 978 1407 11711 9

Printed in the UK by CPI Bookmarque, Croydon, Surrey.
Papers used by Scholastic Children's Books are made from
wood grown in sustainable forests.

1 3 5 7 9 10 8 6 4 2

This is a work of fiction. Names, characters, places,
incidents and dialogues are products of the author's imagination
or are used fictitiously. Any resemblance to actual people, living
or dead, events or locales is entirely coincidental.

www.scholastic.co.uk/zone

With special thanks to Tracey Turner

For Jessica May Cowlard

This Book Belongs To

Beware!
Never open my Book, unless you
want the Curse of Gnome upon you.
Or is it too late?
Then my creatures will terrify
and torment you.
You can't imagine how scared you will be.
Gnome Gardens belongs to me.
Only me. You shall see. . .

CHAPTER ONE

A Creature in the Corridor

"Full steam ahead!" shouted Harry, flicking the switch on his remote control. A model steam train whirred into life and went rattling around the track.

Jamie knelt down next to his brother. Dad had built the train set for them, complete with signals, points, stations, shops and fields of cows. It snaked across and around the whole floor of the den.

"We're coming up Cow Field Straight," Harry said in the booming voice of a TV commentator, his train hurtling along the track past a row of plastic cows, "heading for Danger Corner!"

Jamie braced himself. Harry was going far too fast. Sure enough, as the train took the bend it careered off the track and smashed into Jamie's knees.

"Ow!" Jamie rubbed his leg. "Harry," he said, carefully placing the train back on the tracks, "how many more times? You need to go slower round that bend."

"We should set up a warning system for the trains," said Harry. He dug about in his new backpack. "Look!" he cried, waving a flap of green material. "It's a station master's flag. *And.* . ." He rummaged in the bag again and brought out a shiny object. He put it to his mouth, blew, and the air was split with a piercing shriek.

"*Wheeeeeeee!*"

Jamie covered his ears. "And the world's loudest whistle," he said. "Where did you get that?"

"Village shop," said Harry, looking pleased with himself. "When me and Mum were buying Milly's birthday present. I had some leftover pocket money."

Jamie thought back to Milly's party at her cottage, just down the hill from Gnome Gardens. The kitchen table had been groaning with cake, jelly and ice cream. There were sugar mice and spiders made of liquorice decorating the tabletop. Jamie remembered exchanging glances with Harry and Milly: no one else at the party had the slightest clue that the three of them had met a real-life giant spider, its fangs dripping poison.

A spider was one of the creepy creatures belonging to the evil Gnome. He wanted to scare the boys out of Gnome Gardens so that he could have it all to himself. When they'd last encountered their enemy, they'd left him trapped in a pit of rats. *But he might come back*, Jamie thought.

Harry put down the flag and whistle and rubbed his eyes. For the first time, Jamie noticed the dark rings under them. "You look as if you need some sleep," he said. "Have you been having bad dreams – about the Gnome?"

Harry blushed and started fiddling with the remote control. "No, of course not!" He'd never been any good at lying. Jamie was furious at the thought of the cruel, disgusting little man hurting his younger brother. *We have to stop the Gnome, once and for all,* he thought. He picked up a couple of fallen plastic cows and put them the right way up, then started his own train rolling around the track.

"Remember how the rat helped us last time we met the Gnome?" Jamie said.

Harry nodded.

"Well, maybe the Gnome's creatures don't like him either. They might want to get rid of him too."

"I know the rat helped us," Harry said. "But what about that disgusting snake? What about the spider that trapped us in its sticky web, or the bats that grabbed Milly from her bedroom?"

"You're right," said Jamie. He frowned. "In that case, we'd better make sure we're ready for anything. Let's have a look at *The Book of Gnome* – and find out what it says about the Gnome's next creature."

He pushed a lever on the remote control, steering his train into a siding.

"Do you remember that toad we saw on the lane, after we freed the rat?" asked Harry. "Horrible, warty thing. Maybe the Gnome will send a toad after us. Maybe it'll be a giant one, with a huge long sticky tongue—"

"Let's go and find out, instead of worrying about it," Jamie interrupted.

He stopped his train, stood up and pulled Harry to his feet. They picked their way across the train set to the door. Harry got to it first.

"Race you to the study!" Harry shouted. "Ready, set, GO!" He gave a screeching blast on his whistle and sprinted off down the hall.

Jamie set off after Harry as Mum's voice came echoing through the house. "Harry! Is that you with that whistle?"

They ran up the narrow staircase to the ground floor and along a dingy corridor. Although Mum and Dad had redecorated some of the house, most of the rooms were dusty and neglected. Jamie and Harry had grown used to the cobwebs hanging in corners with fat spiders lurking in them, and the flickering bare light bulbs strung along the ceiling on ancient wires. Even the animal carvings that decorated the woodwork of the house seemed normal now.

Jamie caught up with his brother as they came to the end of a corridor, their trainers squeaking on the floorboards.

"Look out, I'm coming through!" Harry shouted, putting the whistle to his lips.

But as they careered around the corner, something sprang out in front of them. They both skidded to a halt. Harry gave a yelp that turned into a screeching blast on his whistle, and Jamie felt his heart skip as whatever it was landed at their feet with a soft squishing sound.

A small brown creature, covered in bumps. Its bulbous eyes were glinting.

Harry's mouth hung open, the whistle dangling round his neck. He pointed with a trembling finger.

"A toad! Is it the Gnome's creature?"

CHAPTER TWO

The Carvings in the Study

The toad's orange eyes glinted, the skin of its throat pulsing as it breathed. It was about the size of Jamie's palm. With a croak, it hopped on to the toe of one of Jamie's new trainers.

"Ugh!" cried Jamie, shaking his foot.

The toad climbed off and squatted on the

floor, leaving a slimy smudge on the leather. Jamie crouched down and peered closely at the toad, frowning. "I think it's just a toad. An ordinary one, I mean," he said. "Not a creepy creature."

The toad hopped away through a gap in the skirting board, leaving a damp trail across the floor.

Harry's face was white. "But why did it leap out at us like that?"

"Coincidence?" Jamie suggested, trying to smile. But his stomach felt knotted. He knew that creatures didn't just turn up at Gnome Gardens. They were sent by the Gnome.

Jamie led the way down the corridor and into the wood-panelled hallway. He stopped in front of the familiar carving of the Gnome's face, with its scowling expression and large warty nose. "Here we go," he said to Harry, and pressed it. With a groan, the panel next to the face slid back to reveal the dusty secret passage. They walked down it, brushing cobwebs from their path, and into Granddad's old study.

Sunshine poured through the stained-glass skylight, bathing the study in dusty beams of red, green and yellow light – the colours worn by the Gnome. The huge old oak desk, where Granddad had written his books, sat squarely in the middle of the room. Harry knelt beside it and pressed the button that released a secret drawer on top of the desk. The drawer slid open.

Jamie reached inside and took out *The Book of Gnome*, laying it on the desk so that they could both see. The spine of the book creaked as Jamie turned the pages. There was the snake, on the next page was the spider, then the bat, and the rat with its golden crown. The boys glanced at each other, then Jamie turned the page to reveal the Gnome's next creature.

"I was right," said Harry. "It's a toad."

From the middle of the page, two yellow, bulbous eyes stared out at them. The toad's huge, fat body was warty and mottled brown, its wide mouth drawn down at each side. Underneath the picture, in ornate black lettering, was a single sentence.

Jamie read it aloud. "'The key hides in the dark.'" He frowned. "What does *that* mean?"

Harry shrugged. "It's not much of a clue."

Something clattered in the passageway

and they heard footsteps.

Thud. Thud. Thud. Thud.

They stopped outside the study door.

Jamie drew in his breath, staring at Harry. "I think it's the Gnome," he whispered.

Harry gulped and ducked underneath the desk. Jamie darted behind an ancient coal-scuttle by the fireplace.

As well as the footsteps, a humming sound floated from the passageway. "La-la-la-di-da. . ."

"It's Mum!" Harry whispered.

Jamie swallowed. Mum and Dad couldn't find out what they were doing here. They wouldn't believe that an evil Gnome was trying to drive them all out of the house, and attacking them with his creepy creatures – and even if they did, they would probably try to stop the boys and Milly from defeating him.

"Quick!" Jamie hissed. He scrambled out from behind the coal-scuttle and stood in front of the desk, shielding the open *Book of Gnome*. Harry leaped to stand beside him.

The door burst open.

"Didn't expect to find you two in here," said Mum. "Playing hide and seek?"

She was carrying a bucketful of soapy water and a mop. Dad was just behind her, his arms full of dust sheets, cloths, bottles of polish and cleaning fluid.

"Let's clean the room," Dad said, flapping a dust sheet over a moth-eaten green armchair. While Mum helped him, Harry quickly shut *The Book of Gnome* and slid it back in the drawer.

Jamie moved over to one of the bookcases and scanned the shelves, trying to look relaxed. Harry was fiddling with the hem of his T-shirt, looking exactly like he'd been caught in the middle of doing something he shouldn't. Thankfully Mum and Dad didn't seem to have noticed.

"After something to read, then?" Mum asked Jamie.

"Oh, er, yes. . ." Jamie grabbed a book from the shelf at random. "This looks good."

Inside the gap where the book had been, Jamie noticed a dark round disc. At first he thought it was a knot in the wood, but then he saw that it was raised up from the surface of the bookcase, like a button.

"Let's have a look, then," said Dad.

He took the book to the desk and put it down in front of him and Harry, the pages tumbling open.

Dad put his bucket down, reached over and lifted the book cover to look at the title. "*101 Embroidery Stitches*," he read, sounding puzzled. "Are you two thinking of making something?"

Jamie felt his face grow hot. "Well, we were . . . um, just looking something up. For a friend."

Mum narrowed her eyes at Jamie suspiciously. Then she looked around the room.

"Dad and I are going to make a start redecorating. This could be a lovely room," she said. "Even if it *is* a bit . . . odd."

The wood-panelled walls of the study

were covered in carvings of plants and animals. A hawk swooped from the top of one wall, mice and rats scurried lower down, and insects scuttled along the skirting boards. Mum took a pace back from a carving of a wolf, its muzzle drawn into a snarl.

On one of the walls was an oval panel with a snake, a spider, a bat, a rat and a toad carved into it. Each creature had glittering red jewels for eyes. Every time the boys and Milly defeated one of the Gnome's creatures, one of the carvings turned around to face the room. Four of the creatures had moved so far – only the toad was still in profile.

Mum picked up a cloth and strode towards the carvings. "Look at them. They're covered with dust."

Jamie's insides fluttered with worry.

Harry's mouth was gaping open, and he knew his brother was thinking the same thing. *What will happen if Mum touches the carvings?*

Jamie grabbed another book from the shelves. This one was called *Poisonous Fungi*. "Mum, Dad, look here," he said, letting the pages fall open to a picture of a speckled mushroom. "This is called a death cap. Do you think there are any in our garden?"

"Why don't you go and find out?" Mum said, standing in front of the panel. She picked up the end of a long, tasselled rope dangling down to the side of it and frowned.

"Must be for an old servants' bell," said Dad, sloshing water on the floor with his mop.

Jamie glanced at Harry. What were they going to do?

Mum reached out with her duster towards the snake carving and Harry ran over, squeezing himself in front of her.

"You don't need to clean those!" he said.

Mum raised her eyebrows. "Why not?" She gently took Harry by the arms and moved him out of the way.

Harry's face turned pale as Mum gave the snake a vigorous rub with her duster. Jamie held his breath. Mum started humming to herself once more as she carefully polished the snake's jewel eyes, making them glitter even more brightly.

Nothing happened. The carvings didn't move; the Gnome didn't appear.

"Go on, then. Make yourselves scarce," said Dad, leaning on his mop.

Feeling light-headed with relief, Jamie grabbed Harry's hand and pulled him through the study door.

Outside, the grounds of Gnome Gardens were bathed in brilliant sunlight.

"Let's go and find Milly," Jamie said. They set off down a steeply sloping path that snaked across the huge, overgrown garden, past an ancient rockery choked with bindweed. Jamie jumped over a fat black slug oozing across the path. Ahead, a patch of undergrowth trembled. *Is that the Gnome's toad?* he wondered. But instead a jackdaw fluttered out with a low *caw*.

Harry adjusted the straps on his backpack. "I thought the carvings would move when Mum touched them," he said. "What will happen when the toad turns into the room?"

"We still have to defeat it for that to happen," Jamie said.

As he walked, he glanced back at the huge, grey stone house squatting at the top of the hill. It seemed to be staring at them in disapproval. Jamie wished he knew the answer to Harry's question. What *would* happen when there were no creepy creatures left? He shuddered. *Then we'll have to face the Gnome himself. . .*

CHAPTER THREE

Toad Chase

"There's Milly's house," said Jamie, pointing to the red-tiled roof of the Gardener's Cottage, just visible through the trees. "Let's have another race. First to the garden gate wins!"

They hurtled down the path, raced around the dead tree that had been struck by lightning, jumped a low, crumbling wall, and ran past the long-abandoned greenhouse with its shattered panes.

"Come on, Harry – keep up!" Jamie teased as he dashed ahead of his brother.

They zigzagged between the trees in the old apple orchard, dodging their gnarled branches and the fruit buzzing with wasps. Jamie shuddered as he passed the old stone well, leaning at a dangerous angle. He remembered the stone snakes on its rim squirming into life during their first encounter with the Gnome.

A bright flash of light caught Jamie's eye. The sunshine was glinting on something to his left. He slowed and turned to look. It was a pond, half-hidden by overgrown bushes and tall weeds. He'd never seen it before.

He stopped suddenly, sending Harry crashing into his back.

"Why'd you stop?" Harry panted. "Worried I'd beat you again?"

Jamie pointed at the pool of water.

"A pond!" said Harry, smiling. "I've never been in that bit of the garden before."

They hurried towards it, pushing through enormous, sprawling brambles and stinging nettles that reached Jamie's shoulders.

At the water's edge, Jamie felt thick mud sucking at his trainers. "It's almost big enough to swim in," Jamie said. He covered his nose with his hand. "Not that anyone would want to."

A rotten smell seemed to rise like steam from the pond's surface. The water was covered in green algae and stringy pond weed. Flies buzzed above it in small black clouds. There were a few lily pads, but the leaves were a sickly yellow and they didn't have any flowers.

"Phew! Why does it smell so bad?" Harry asked, wafting a hand in front of his face.

"Because the water's stagnant," said a voice behind them. "It's gone off like rotten food."

"Milly!" Jamie said with a grin.

"It needs clearing out. My dad would know how to do it," Milly's voice continued. "He knows everything."

Jamie glanced at Harry, sharing a secret smile. *So* that's *where she gets it from*, he thought. Milly liked to think she knew everything about everything.

Their friend emerged from behind the

reeds and nettles, her jeans tucked into her wellies. "Hang on," she said. "What's that?"

She squelched through the boggy ground to one side of them, the mud slopping up her boots. Jamie and Harry squelched after her. She was pointing to something at the edge of the pond, a few strides away from them, surrounded by reeds.

Jamie peered into the shadows. It was a great lump of stone, taller than him and much wider.

"It's just a massive rock," he said. The three of them moved closer, parting the reeds to see it more clearly. Dappled sunlight fell on something that looked like a giant eye, surrounded by warty skin. Jamie felt the hairs on the back of his neck stand up.

"It's a statue," he said, swallowing hard. "Of a toad."

"Look at its mouth," said Harry, his voice quavering. "It could swallow us whole. If it was real."

A breeze shook the branches overhead, making shadows ripple across the surface of the statue. Jamie gasped. The statue was moving. There were small, warty bodies all over it, squirming and writhing over one another.

"It's made out of toads," Milly said hoarsely. "Real ones."

Ribbit! A rasping croak sounded.

For a moment the three of them stood staring, frozen with fear. One of the toads whipped its tongue into the air, snatching a fly. Its bulging eyes swivelled towards them.

Then it leaped down, hopping forward on powerful back legs. Another toad followed. Then another.

"Run!" shouted Jamie. The three of them turned and crashed back through the nettles and brambles.

"There're hundreds of them!" Harry shouted.

Jamie glanced behind him to see a mass of warty brownish creatures advancing on them like a river of boiling mud. These weren't ordinary toads. They were moving too quickly, springing forward as fast as Jamie could run. *They must be the Gnome's*, he thought.

Thorny brambles snatched at Jamie's clothes. He winced as a tall nettle stung the side of his face. As he leaped over a rotting log, he saw the boundary of their garden ahead of them, marked by a deep ditch and an ancient, dilapidated fence.

"We'll never get past that!" Milly cried, her hair streaming behind her.

"The toads will get us!" whimpered Harry.

Jamie looked around desperately. He could hear the rasping croaks of the toads behind them. Not far away, part of the fence had come down. They would just have to jump the ditch.

"This way!" he panted, running towards the broken section.

"We'll need a run-up to get over that ditch," Milly said. "Come on!"

She put on a burst of speed and sailed over the ditch, her arms wide in the air, legs tucked up beneath her.

Jamie paused, drew in his breath and

leaped across after her. The stream of brown water and matted grass at the bottom of the ditch flashed past underneath him. He landed on his hands and knees at the other side, next to the broken fence. He turned to look for his brother.

"Catch me, Jamie!" Harry shouted as he came sprinting towards the ditch. He jumped, his arms flapping . . . but not quite far enough. He thudded into the side of the ditch, his legs dangling. With a chorus of grunts and croaks, the toads leaped in after him, their long tongues flickering.

Harry's face was white as he struggled to find a toehold in the warty skin of the toads that were wriggling below. Jamie flung himself flat on the bank, stretching out a hand towards him.

"Hold on!" he said.

Harry's fingers closed around his. Jamie heaved, Milly kneeling down to help, and they dragged Harry away from the toads and on to the bank.

The three of them scrambled to their feet, covered in mud. "Ugh!" Harry cried, looking down at his jeans. They were smeared with the toads' glistening slime.

The bottom of the ditch was full of toads now, writhing about, struggling to climb the steep, slippery sides.

"Quick!" said Milly. "It won't be long before they get out."

They squeezed through the gap in the fence, the jagged wood catching on their clothes, and emerged into a large, muddy field ringed by wooden fences. *Keeping something in or something out?* wondered Jamie.

There was a stone water trough at the side of the field, shaded by a copse of trees, and a huge oak tree stood in the middle. There was a sign on its trunk. They ran over to read it:

DANGER!
OLD MINE SHAFTS

"Mine shafts?" said Harry. "Is that what those fences are for?"

"I bet they are," said Milly. "Digging out mines makes the ground above them weak. Those fences are to stop people walking on the dangerous parts."

Jamie looked at the muddy grass and

gulped. The ground might give way at any moment.

"There's a story about a mine under Gnome Gardens," Milly continued. She looked at Jamie and Harry. "A gold mine. I thought it was just a legend . . . until now."

"Gold! The Gnome's favourite thing in the whole world," Harry said.

"The story says that the mines were abandoned," Milly said. "There can't be any gold left."

The field shuddered with the sound of rasping croaks. They froze.

"Oh no," Harry said, his eyes wide.

The snap of splintering wood made them turn towards the fence. The mass of toads was pressing against it, squirming and wriggling, making panels fall down. To Jamie's horror, their warty bodies seemed to melt, blurring and fusing together to form one enormous toad. It was as tall as the fence, its skin covered in scabs and slime. Its yellow eyes blinked and its tongue slithered in and out of its mouth, oozing with drool.

"It's like the snakes," Jamie said, shaking. "All those little creatures turning into a massive, horrible one."

"That's right!" cackled a voice from behind the fence. "Clever little children, aren't you? But not clever enough to defeat me!"

The Gnome.

Jamie felt Harry grip his sleeve. Milly took a step back.

Through the gap in the fence, they saw the scrawny little Gnome beside the giant toad. His red cap was greasy and a wispy beard sprouted from his chin. He grinned, revealing pointy yellow teeth.

The Gnome leaped on to the toad's back. "Attack!" he yelled.

The creature charged towards them, springing across the field in massive bounds.

Fear clenched inside Jamie. This time, there was no escape. . .

CHAPTER FOUR

The Monstrous Toad

Jamie whirled around.

"Get behind the trough!" he shouted. He grabbed Harry by his backpack with one hand and Milly's arm with the other, and pulled them across the field. They crouched low to the ground, ducking behind trees and bushes. The mud became thicker the closer they got to the water trough, and when they ducked down behind it, it was like sitting in a vat of baked beans.

"Did the Gnome see where we went?" whimpered Harry. Mud covered his clothes and splattered his face and hair. Milly's face and body were smeared in patches of thick brown mud, except for two pale ovals where her eyes were.

Jamie peered around the edge of the trough.

The giant toad crouched in the mud by one of the rings of fences. It was only a few paces away, and Jamie could see every bump of its warty brown skin. Its yellow eyes flicked to and fro, following the movement of a buzzing wasp. Quick as a whip, it shot its long, sticky tongue high into the air and drew the insect into its huge mouth. It chewed lazily, blinking its yellow eyes. The Gnome patted its slimy head as he peered around the field.

"They haven't seen us," Jamie whispered.

"OK," Milly said. "Now we need to work out how to defeat the Gnome. Harry, what have you got in your backpack?"

Harry turned round, sloshing in the mud, so Milly and Jamie could look inside. But when he leaned forward against the trough it gave a loud crack and split apart, releasing a cascade of green rainwater.

The Gnome's head snapped round towards the noise. He slipped down from the toad's back on to the muddy ground, craning his scrawny neck as he tried to spot them. His eyes glinted red as they met Jamie's and his mouth twisted into an ugly smile.

"Fools! Did you think you'd seen the last of me?" the Gnome shouted, rubbing his hands together. His twisted yellow nails were almost as long as the fingers and the tips were jagged and sharp. "You left me in that pit of rats, but now I'm back. And I want revenge!"

"We're not scared of you, Gnome!" Jamie shouted, though his heart thudded violently in his chest.

The Gnome's face was red with fury as he turned his horrible gaze from Jamie to Harry to Milly. "Let me introduce you to my creature," he sneered, calmer now. "Lovely, isn't he? My favourite creature of all." The

Gnome patted the thick folds of the toad's warty skin.

The toad eyed them steadily, shifting on its muscular back legs.

"Now, creature!" the Gnome commanded.

Snap! The revolting sticky tongue darted out of the toad's mouth. It was enormous – longer than a skipping rope. In one swift movement it curled around Jamie, Harry and Milly, yanking them together and holding them fast. Jamie felt a wave of nausea as the slimy muscle tightened its grip. The toad dragged them through the mud, back towards its gaping mouth.

"It's going to eat us!" screamed Harry.

Milly pushed frantically at the horrible pink tongue. "Let go of us, you disgusting thing!" she cried. Her hands were covered in strands of the toad's saliva.

Jamie struggled, thumping at the tongue, but it slid steadily back down the toad's throat. Its huge open jaws loomed closer, like the mouth of a cave, dripping slimy drool into the mud.

"No!" shouted Harry. He was sobbing with fear.

"Nearly there!" laughed the Gnome. He was dancing around them, splashes of mud covering his clothes and the small silver hammer that hung from his belt. They were a heartbeat away from that slimy, gaping mouth. Jamie closed his eyes. He felt himself being lifted up. He waited for the toad's jaws to clamp down on him.

This is it, he thought. *The Gnome has won.*

Suddenly, he was plunging downwards. His eyes snapped open. They hadn't been swallowed by the toad! Through the darkness he could hear the screams of Harry and Milly joining his own, as they bumped and slithered down a steep muddy tunnel. As he twisted and tumbled, he caught a glimpse of the Gnome's ugly face leering down at him, grinning with delight, the toad peering over his shoulder.

They landed in a heap on a dirt floor.

Jamie struggled to his feet. "Are you two all right?"

"No," said Harry. "I've just been slobbered on by a giant toad."

"I'm fine," Milly said.

Jamie could hardly see their muddy faces in the gloom – just the whites of their eyes. As his sight adjusted to the dark, he looked up at the tunnel they had come down. "This must be one of the old mine shafts," he said.

Milly dusted herself off. "Now, how are we going to get out of here?"

They were standing in the middle of a huge cavern. In the dim light, Jamie could make out that the walls around them were streaked with gold.

"The mines aren't empty after all," Harry said.

Jamie peered at the shining metal. It reminded him of something, but he couldn't think what.

Hiiiiiiiiiiissssssssssssssssss. . .

They all three froze. "What was that?" asked Harry, his voice trembling.

There was another hiss, then a scratching sound came from somewhere among the shadows. As his eyes adjusted to the darkness, Jamie saw chambers cut into the walls, with a wooden post outside each one. Attached to the posts were greasy ropes that looked as though they were made from human hair. And tied to the ropes . . . were the Gnome's creepy creatures.

The giant snake lay tightly coiled, its head drooping on the ground, its tongue tasting the air. The bat hung upside down from a ledge inside its chamber, wrapped in its leathery wings. The spider squatted on the sticky web it had woven, two of its legs injured from the fight they'd had. Finally

Jamie looked at the King Rat, no longer wearing its golden crown, whimpering as it struggled against the rope. They'd helped it to escape from the Gnome . . . or so Jamie had thought.

All around the chamber was a horrible smell. The scent of fear.

"The poor things," said Milly. "They're scared."

The creatures stared out at them in silent appeals for help.

A cackle echoed from behind. "So, you've already met your fellow prisoners," said the Gnome.

With an oozing splat, the giant toad dropped down the mineshaft, landing in the mud at the bottom. The Gnome was sitting on its back.

Jamie, Harry and Milly drew closer together.

"You can't keep us prisoner, Gnome," said Jamie, sounding much braver than he felt.

"Can't I?" The Gnome spat on the floor. "Look over there."

He pointed to a corner where there was an empty chamber in the cave wall. In front of it were three wooden posts, and three slimy hair ropes.

"Welcome to your new home," he sneered, rubbing his hands together. "You'll never see Gnome Gardens again!"

CHAPTER FIVE

The Cavern of Creatures

"Attack!" the Gnome yelled at the toad, digging his feet into the creature's warty flank.

The toad gave a deep croak, its red jaws gaping. But it didn't move.

The Gnome jumped off and picked up one of the greasy ropes. He slapped it against the toad. "Come on, you stupid creature! Get them!"

A growl like a bubbling drain sounded from the toad's throat. Its eyes narrowed to angry slits and it opened its mouth wide, flicking an enormous tongue at the Gnome.

"Not me!" the Gnome screeched, scurrying away from the rippling pink coil.

Jamie could see Milly's eyes shining in the darkness. "The toad's on our side," she said.

As the Gnome jumped and ran around the cavern, dodging the toad's attacks, Jamie turned to Harry. "What's in your backpack?" he whispered.

Harry unzipped it with trembling fingers, his eyes on the battling Gnome and toad.

Jamie thrust his hand inside. He felt a rolled-up pair of socks, a comic, and a packet of toffees. Then his hand clasped around a long, thin stick with a triangle of fabric attached to the end.

"The station master's flag," Jamie said, pulling it out. "That won't help us."

The Gnome whirled the length of rope over his head like a lasso, swinging it at the toad. The creature's tongue shot out but the rope snared around it. The toad gave a croak of pain.

"Got you!" the Gnome shrieked with delight.

"Are you sure there isn't anything else?" Milly hissed to Harry.

Harry rummaged around at the bottom of the backpack and pulled out the whistle.

Jamie's shoulders drooped. "We haven't got anything that will help us this time."

The Gnome yanked on the rope, dragging the toad by its tongue towards the empty cell. "You've betrayed me too," he snarled. "You can stay here with these filthy brats."

"Oh no," said Harry, his eyes wide. "We're never going to escape."

"Wait!" Milly hissed. "The whistle. Think about how it works."

"What do you mean?" whispered Jamie.

"Don't you know?" Milly replied. "There's a ball bearing inside it. That's what makes the sound. We could use the flag to make a catapult and fire the ball bearing at the Gnome."

Jamie thought it sounded like the worst

plan he'd ever heard. But the Gnome was already knotting the toad's tongue to the wooden post next to the empty cell. If they didn't do something, they'd be trapped here with his creatures.

He gave Milly a hesitant thumbs up. "It's the best idea we have," he admitted. He looked down at the shiny whistle in his palm. "OK, then. We need to break this to get the ball bearing out."

The toad strained against the post, trying to undo the knot in its tongue. Cackling with glee, the Gnome scampered across the cavern. He cracked the rope like a whip. "Now it's your turn to go inside the cell," he sneered, his eyes glinting at them.

As he passed the snake it reared up with

a loud, rasping hiss. The huge creature had its mouth open, its glistening fangs dripping poison. Then suddenly it lunged at the Gnome, pulling its rope as far as it would go. He darted aside and the snake's jaws snapped shut on empty air.

"It's attacking him!" Milly cried.

"Back, creature!" shouted the Gnome.

He cracked the rope at Harry. It caught on his shoulder and Harry yelped and leaped backwards, dropping the whistle on the ground. It skittered across the floor.

"No!" yelled Jamie. He dived after it, but the Gnome thwacked the rope on the ground, blocking his path. The whistle came to a rest in front of the rat's cell.

"Spoiled your silly little plan, did I?" said

the Gnome, pretending to wipe tears from his eyes. "Boo, hoo, hoo."

Behind the Gnome, Jamie could see the rat's eyes glittering in the darkness. It picked up the whistle in its huge yellow teeth and crunched down on it. *It's as if it knows what we're trying to do*, Jamie thought.

Snap. The rat's teeth broke the whistle in half. The ball bearing came flying out, sailing through the air.

Jamie sprinted towards it, his hands outstretched like he was making a catch in a game of cricket. His hands clasped over the metal ball.

"Where do you think you're going?" snarled the Gnome. He spun towards Jamie, raising the rope, ready to strike.

Milly waved her arms above her head. "Over here!" she yelled to the Gnome. She ran towards the snake. Harry pulled the station master's flag out of his backpack and tossed it to Jamie. Then he ran after Milly.

They're distracting the Gnome, Jamie realized. He felt a swell of pride at how brave they were.

"What are you up to now?" the Gnome spat, swivelling around towards Milly and Harry. He swiped at them with his bony, clawlike hand. Harry had to jump backwards and the Gnome's filthy yellow nails sliced into the snake's wooden post, leaving a deep slash.

Jamie folded the stretchy cloth of the flag in half to make a catapult. He tucked the ball bearing inside it and moved around the cavern, waiting for the right moment to fire it at the Gnome. *If only there was more light,* he thought, *it would make it easier to see where the target is.* The only light came from the opening to the mine shaft above them. As Jamie skirted around the walls of the cavern, he noticed that a shaft of light was reflecting on the threads of gold in the cave walls, making them glimmer in the darkness.

The dark. . . He remembered the clue in *The Book of Gnome. The key lies in the dark!*

"Look for a key!" he shouted to Harry and Milly.

"Idiots!" spat the Gnome. He laughed, a sound that sent shivers down Jamie's spine. "You haven't got a clue!"

The snake darted its head at the Gnome

again, its fangs dripping.

"Stupid creature!" shouted the Gnome, striking its neck with the rope.

The snake hissed furiously and the other creatures strained against their ropes, struggling and thrashing. The toad flicked its pink tongue, and Jamie noticed that it had almost freed itself.

"Come and get me – if you can!" Jamie shouted to the Gnome. He crouched on the floor, his eyes fixed on the Gnome's bony legs.

The Gnome whirled the rope above his head. "Oh, I'll get you, all right," he snarled. The Gnome drew back his lips into a horrible cry of rage and raced at him.

Jamie pulled back the catapult and let go.

The ball bearing hurtled through the air towards the Gnome. *Please, let this work*, Jamie thought. *It's our only hope. . .*

CHAPTER SIX

The Creatures Advance

The Gnome ran towards Jamie, the rope swooping above him, his cracked lips drawn back in a triumphant laugh.

Thwack!

The ball bearing struck the Gnome in the middle of his forehead. He dropped the rope and clasped his hands to his face. Giddily, he staggered about in circles. Jamie dodged out of his path.

"Curses!" the Gnome screeched.

"Go, Jamie!" cried Harry, punching the air.

With an echoing croak, the toad yanked its tongue free. Its huge bulbous eyes swivelled towards the Gnome.

The evil little man tipped back . . . back . . . He gave a shrill shriek as he crashed to the ground.

The toad bounded at the Gnome. Its tongue lashed out at him, leaving a trail of slime across his face. "Aarrgh!" cried the Gnome, wriggling away. "Don't attack me, you fool!" He reached out and bashed its shoulder with his fist. The toad flinched. "Fool!" shouted the Gnome again.

The word echoed around the cavern. Jamie struggled to think. *Fool*. What did it remind him of?

The light from the top of the mine shaft made the walls glitter with gold. *That's it!* Jamie thought. He'd seen a TV programme about a mine that had been full of *fool*'s gold.

The Gnome staggered to his feet. "You'll pay for this, you stupid creature," he muttered viciously to the toad. "And so will the three of you." He jabbed a bony finger at Harry and Milly. "But especially *you*," he snarled, pointing at Jamie.

Jamie was racking his brain. The professor in the TV programme had explained how to tell if shiny yellow metal was gold or not. *Fool's gold is made up of hundreds of little cubes*, Jamie remembered. He backed against the cave wall and felt in the rock for one of the seams of metal. He placed his hand against it. He could trace tiny squares with his fingertips.

The Gnome was advancing on Harry and Milly. He rolled up his sleeves. "I'll put you in the cells with my bare hands," he growled. "Little fools."

Jamie burst into laughter.

The Gnome swung round. "What have *you* got to be so pleased about?" he snapped.

"*You're* the fool, Gnome," Jamie said.

"What?" The Gnome's eyes blazed with fury.

"This is fool's gold." Jamie put a hand to the rock behind him. "It's just a cheap metal. All this time, you've been protecting a worthless mine."

"You're lying!" screeched the Gnome. His face was purple, his hands clenched into fists.

"Real gold is nothing like this. Don't you know anything?" said Jamie.

"He's right," Milly said, looking at the cave wall. She ran her hand over the shiny surface. "Scientists call it pyrite. It's not worth anything."

"You're lying!" spat the Gnome. The veins on his scrawny arms and neck stood out like string. He took the hammer from his belt and bashed it at the cave. "It's real! Pure gold!" he snarled as he hacked at the rock. Lumps of shining square-shaped crystals tumbled from the wall as he hit it.

Harry was on his hands and knees, searching the floor. "I can't see a key anywhere," he said. "What would we use one for anyway?"

"Maybe it's not *literally* a key that we need to find," said Milly. "Maybe the creatures are the key! The rat rescued us before. Maybe they'll all help this time."

"We'd have to free them to find out," Jamie said.

Harry looked nervously towards the giant spider, which was baring its fangs. "What if they attack us again?" he said.

The Gnome gave a furious cry and hurled the silver hammer towards them. The toad's tongue flashed out, wrapping round the hammer before it could strike Jamie's head. With a deep croak, it threw the hammer back at the Gnome. He gave a squawk of surprise, jumping from its path. The hammer struck the wall, sending down a shower of crystals.

"You're right, Milly," Jamie cried. "It's not us the creatures will attack – it's the Gnome. Let's free them!"

The Gnome advanced towards the three of them. "You don't know what you're talking about!" he said. He made a lunge at Harry. His clawlike fingernails swished through the air as Harry leaped backwards. The filthy nails were sharp. . . *Sharp enough to cut through rope?* Jamie wondered.

"His nails," he whispered to Harry and Milly. "We have to make him attack us near the ropes. Get him to cut through them with his nails."

Milly and Harry both nodded.

"I'll go first," said Harry. He darted

towards the rope that tethered the bat, his backpack bouncing.

The Gnome swerved after him. "Come back!" he snarled.

He ran at Harry, slashing at him with his nails. Harry neared the bat's rope and leaped up to vault over it, but the Gnome caught him up. Jamie went cold. As the Gnome threw himself at Harry the toad bounded forward. Its tongue whipped out and snatched him clear of the Gnome.

The Gnome tumbled on to the rope, his nails almost cutting through it completely.

The toad carefully placed Harry on the ground beside Jamie and Milly. Apart from a long tear in his backpack, he was OK.

"Um, thanks," said Harry, patting the

toad's slimy nose. The creature's bulging eyes blinked at him.

The Gnome scrambled to his feet. "Bat!" he shouted. "Attack them!"

The giant bat let go of the ledge inside its shell. It flapped its vast leathery wings to flip itself over, standing on its feet. It screeched at the Gnome and started tugging at the damaged rope.

"They won't do what you say any more, Gnome!" Jamie called.

Milly scooped up a piece of the fool's gold the Gnome had chipped from the wall. "Take that!" she shouted, throwing it at him. It glanced off the Gnome's shoulder.

"How dare you!" the Gnome shouted, circling his rope in the air like a lasso. He swung it towards Milly, but she nimbly jumped out of the way. The Gnome wheeled round after her. She dodged his blows, spinning out of the Gnome's path so his nails slashed at the spider's rope, fraying its greasy strands.

The spider hissed and tugged at the rope. It wasn't coming loose – yet. Jamie and Harry shared a glance, then Harry leaped past the snake's rope, so that the Gnome lunged after him. As he snatched at Harry, his nails neatly slashed the rope in two. The snake was free!

Now for the rat, Jamie thought.

"Over here, Gnome!" Jamie shouted, waving his arms close to the rat's rope.

"You stupid child!" the Gnome snarled. "You can't dodge me for ever!" He launched himself at Jamie and his filthy nails slashed downwards, tearing Jamie's T-shirt and painfully scratching his skin.

"Jamie!" cried Harry.

"Got you!" shouted the Gnome triumphantly.

Jamie bit his lip, clutching his shoulder.

"Leave my brother alone," Harry shouted. He ran towards the Gnome. The Gnome lunged at him – and Harry scrambled under the rope that secured the rat. The Gnome tried to attack again and his nails ripped the rope almost in two.

"Ha! Missed me!" shouted Harry, sprinting away. The Gnome followed, his face twisted with rage.

Jamie picked up the frayed rope holding the rat. He yanked it, his shoulders straining, as if he were fighting the wooden post in a tug-of-war. With a tearing sound, the greasy strands parted and fell to the floor.

The rat licked its huge yellow teeth. Its eyes seemed to shine with gratitude.

Jamie spun round. "Harry! Milly! Release the other creatures!"

The rat and the toad advanced on the Gnome, as if they knew to keep him distracted. "Traitors!" the Gnome screeched, retreating back against the glittering walls.

Jamie pulled at the last strands of the spider's rope. It hissed and marched to join the toad and the rat. Harry used a shard of fool's gold to work on the bat's rope, while Milly took the snake's, tearing at it with her fingers. As their bonds fell away, the bat swooped to hover above the Gnome, while the snake reared up beside him.

"No!" shouted the Gnome. He was pressed back against the wall, surrounded. He pointed a quivering finger at the three friends. "Attack them! Kill them! Suck their blood and gnaw their bones!"

The snake's head swivelled to look at them. It bared its fangs and hissed. The other four creatures turned round too, their eyes fixed on Jamie, Harry and Milly.

Jamie gulped. Would the creatures attack them after all?

CHAPTER SEVEN

Spider Ride

"What are you waiting for?" shouted the Gnome. "Attack!"

None of the creatures moved.

"Do as I say!" the Gnome screeched. He picked up a lump of fool's gold in each hand and used them to hit the snake and the bat squarely on the side of the head. The bat squealed in pain.

Slowly, its forked tongue darting from its mouth, the snake turned back to face the Gnome. Then the bat turned its ugly snout to look at him. The spider moved round, then the toad, and lastly the rat, the fur on its spine standing rigid.

The Gnome's face was purple with rage. "You'll regret this," he said to the creatures. Then he pointed a bony finger at Jamie. "You won't defeat me," he said. "I've not finished with you yet."

He slipped between the bat and the snake and made a dash for the mine shaft.

"Quick! Don't let him get away!" shouted Milly.

She, Jamie and Harry chased after him. The Gnome scrabbled at the sides of the shaft, gripping the lumpy rock with his long nails. He looked down at them, grinning. "Bye, silly brats!"

But as he clambered up the shaft, the bat swooped towards him. It screeched and struck the Gnome with one of its leathery wings, toppling him to the ground. He landed with a squelch in the mud.

"Curse you!" the Gnome shrieked.

The toad hopped towards him and flicked out its squishy tongue. It wrapped around the Gnome and flipped him over and over, winding him in oozy pink coils. Then the toad dragged him upright and gripped him in its jaws.

The rat looked at Jamie, its whiskers twitching, then set off, sniffing the ground, into the darkness at the other side of the cavern. It disappeared behind a big rock.

"There must be a way out over there," Jamie said. "Come on – I think the rat wants us to follow it."

The three of them hurried after the rat. The toad hopped behind them, the wriggling Gnome in its mouth. The snake brought up the rear and the bat flapped above them as they entered a tunnel. For the first time in weeks, Jamie didn't feel scared of the creatures. *They're on our side!* he thought, his heart swelling with pride.

Then Jamie heard a scuttling sound; he looked back to see the spider running up the tunnel wall and along the ceiling, flashing over the gleaming patches of fool's gold. It easily overtook the other creatures, despite its injured legs. It dropped down on a length of sticky web, landing in front of Jamie, Harry and Milly.

"What does it want?" asked Harry. The other creatures paused, watching them too.

The spider bent its legs so that its body was closer to the floor. Its jaws were closed. Its eight eyes glittered in the golden light from the walls.

"It wants to give us a ride!" Milly realized. "Do you think that's a good idea?"

Jamie reached out a hand and put it on one of the spider's thick, hairy legs. He tensed his muscles, ready to run if the spider turned on him. But the creature didn't move. Jamie grasped the leg with his other hand and hauled himself up, on to its back.

"Come on," Jamie told the others. "It isn't going to hurt us." The coarse hair that covered the spider's body prickled against his legs.

Harry grabbed the spider's side, heaving himself to sit next to him. Milly scrambled up beside them.

"I never thought we'd be getting a lift from a giant spider!" she said.

The spider scuttled off down the tunnel, breaking into a lopsided run, all the other creatures hurrying beside it. The musty air in the mine rushed past Jamie's ears. He had to grab on to the spider's hairs to stop himself from falling off as they bumped along, ducking their heads beneath the low tunnel roof.

"This is brilliant!" shouted Milly.

"Wait till we tell Mum and Dad!" said Harry. "Oh. Maybe not," he added. His backpack bounced against his back with every jolt of the spider's uneven stride.

"Put me down, creature!" the Gnome shrieked.

Jamie glanced over his shoulder. The Gnome was struggling in the toad's mouth as the creature hopped along. By the dim light of the fool's gold, his face was a shadowy mask of rage. Flecks of spittle had collected in the corners of his mouth.

"You're in my house," yelled the Gnome. "You've stolen it from me. You've stolen my treasure. Mark my words – you will pay."

But Jamie could hear the desperation in the Gnome's voice. *He knows he's losing.*

The tunnel narrowed, tapering down to a dead end. The creatures stopped. Set into the ceiling was a trapdoor. The rat sat up on its haunches, sniffing at the wooden surface. It pushed at the trapdoor with its nose. With a squeak of rusty hinges, it swung open.

The bat swooped up through it and out of sight. The rat sprang up, its claws scratching the edge of the doorway as it scrambled through. The snake slithered up through the door, then the toad hopped through in one leap, the Gnome struggling in its grasp.

"Whoa!" shouted Jamie, lurching backwards as the spider scurried up the wall of the tunnel. He, Harry and Milly hung upside down for a while as the spider moved across the ceiling. The blood rushed to Jamie's head as he clung on tightly to the creature's bristly back. Then the spider shot through the trapdoor.

Jamie blinked in the sudden brightness. Flashes of red, green and yellow light danced in front of his eyes. He gave a gasp of astonishment.

"We're in the study," he said.

The trapdoor had opened right next to the desk in the centre of the room. Jamie climbed down from the spider's back, giving the creature a gentle pat. The mop leaned against the desk, the bucket and duster beside it on the floor. Thankfully, there was no sign of Mum and Dad.

The creatures crowded inside the room, the bat hanging upside down from the skylight. The Gnome kicked furiously, his gnarled feet slamming against the toad's side. The toad's eyes narrowed angrily and it tossed its head, shaking the Gnome to a blur.

"We've got to do something with him, quickly," Milly said. "Your mum and dad could come in at any moment."

Jamie looked desperately around the room for something that might help. He tugged at the tasselled bell-rope, wondering if they could use it as a gag, but it was securely fixed to the ceiling.

"Fools!" the Gnome shouted, his voice hoarse from shrieking. "I'll get you. I'll get the lot of you!"

He thrashed in the toad's grip, scissoring his legs and slashing at it with his nails. With a grunt of pain, the toad unravelled its tongue and the Gnome sprang free. He leaped on to the desk, whipping something from his pocket.

"Get back, all of you!" he snarled. A sharp blade glinted red in his bony hand.

CHAPTER EIGHT

The Golden Touch

The Gnome swished the knife in front of him. The blade was even longer and sharper than his filthy nails.

Jamie, Harry and Milly stared wide-eyed, frozen with horror. The rat crept slowly towards him, baring its teeth.

"I said, get back!" shouted the Gnome.

He lunged forward and the tip of his knife sliced through one of the rat's whiskers.

Harry gasped, his face pale. "He's hurting the rat, Jamie."

The snake was slithering behind the desk, where the Gnome couldn't see it. It moved slowly, silently, until it was close to the Gnome's back. Then it moved lightning fast, bashing the Gnome's hand with a flick of its muscular tail. The knife spun from his grasp and skittered across the floor.

"Curse you! Traitor!" shouted the Gnome. He leaped from the desk after the knife, but the rat batted it with its paw. The knife fell down the trapdoor.

The creatures surrounded the Gnome,

backing him into a corner of the study, against one of the bookcases.

"What now?" said Harry.

"There must be a reason why the creatures brought us here," Jamie said. "If only they could tell us."

"We've got to think logically," Milly said. "There must be something in this room – another secret passageway, maybe."

"The passageway into this study's behind a carving of the Gnome's face," Jamie remembered. "Is there another one somewhere?"

They looked around the room. There were carvings all over the place. Milly and Harry scanned the walls too, examining the wooden panelling carefully, pressing it here and there.

"Boys!" Mum's voice echoed from somewhere in the house.

Jamie, Harry and Milly stared at one another in horror.

"We've got to move fast," said Jamie.

He felt the carving of a hare sitting next to a thorn bush. The branches of the bush curled up to meet the edge of one of the bookcases. Suddenly Jamie remembered grabbing the embroidery book and the strange knot in the gap, like a button.

He raced across the room behind the desk and quickly found the empty space in the bookshelves. Yes: there was a wooden button at the back, shaped like an old-fashioned doorbell. He reached out and pressed it.

Nothing.

"Let me go, you traitors!" shrieked the Gnome. The rat squealed in pain as the Gnome scratched at it with his nails.

Jamie's heart was thumping. *Please do something,* he thought. He pressed the button again, much harder this time.

Click. With a groan, the bookshelf began to slide slowly to one side.

"Jamie? What is it?" called Milly. She and Harry rushed to his side.

They gasped. As the bookcase moved, a golden glow spread into the room. Behind it was a chamber with another tall bookcase. But this one was made of shining, bright gold.

"What's that?" said the Gnome.

The creatures moved aside and he stepped

towards it. His mouth was open. A trail of drool dangled from his cracked lips, and his eyes were wide. "Gold!" he gasped, rubbing his hands.

Jamie, Harry and Milly peered inside. The shelves were lined with golden books. From one of them, a golden spider dangled from a shining thread, its front legs raised, as if it had been frozen in time.

"That's definitely not fool's gold," Jamie whispered. Harry and Milly's faces were bathed in its yellow glow.

The Gnome stumbled towards the chamber. He reached towards the glowing books, his clawlike hand trembling.

"It's mine," the Gnome said. "All mine!"

His fingers closed around the spine of a

book. The tips of his fingers became golden, as if the gold were seeping into his skin. It crept up his arm, across his shoulders, down his bony body to his toes. He stiffened and froze.

"He's turning to gold," Milly gasped.

The gold seeped up his neck. His wispy beard became metal threads and his greasy skin turned yellow.

"My treasure," the Gnome whispered, "at last."

He looked over his shoulder to send the three friends an evil grin. But then his smile faltered as he realized what was happening.

"You've defeated me this time," he said, "but this isn't the end. . ."

Before he could say another word, the

golden glow reached his lips, silencing them for ever.

Jamie and the others stood in stunned silence for a few moments.

"He's turned into a statue," said Harry eventually.

Jamie peered round the golden bookcase. It was part of a whole golden room lined with books and a golden table, a gleaming bowl of fruit on top. And there were other golden Gnomes, frozen as they reached towards the bookshelf. One was reaching high up, standing on tiptoes, his fingers outstretched, the tip of his bushy beard touching the shelf. Another had his hands out straight in front of him, clasping two of the shining books. The Gnomes' faces were full of greed.

"Golden statues," whispered Milly. "Frozen in time."

"So there were other Gnomes," Harry said. "All of them greedy."

Jamie reached for the wooden button and pressed it again. The bookcase slid back into place, concealing the golden room.

He grinned at the others. "We did it. We defeated the Gnome!"

The five creatures nudged against them in celebration. The spider waved its legs, while the bat swooped around the high ceiling. Then, with a croak, the toad hopped down inside the trapdoor. The snake slithered after it, then the spider and the bat. The rat nodded at them before it leaped down, as if it was saying goodbye. Jamie held his hand up to it in farewell.

Jamie, Harry and Milly knelt on the ground, heaving the wooden trapdoor shut.

The study was silent.

The three friends looked at one another.

"Is that it?" Harry asked. "No more Gnome? No more creepy creatures?"

"It's like it never happened," Milly said. She felt the smooth surface of the floor. "I can't even see where the trapdoor was."

"Look," said Harry, pointing at the oval panel mounted on the wall. They had changed into a ring of carved flowers, a red jewel at the centre of each.

Footsteps echoed outside the study. The door swung open and Mum peered inside. "I've been looking for you," she said. "What was all that noise about?"

Jamie, Harry and Milly stared at one another.

Mum came inside the room, humming to herself, and picked up the duster. She shook it out and stepped towards the oval panel. Her eyes opened wide in surprise. "Oh, you've cleaned it for me! They were so covered in dust, they looked like horrible creatures before. Creepy."

"They certainly were," said Jamie. "But they've gone now."

Harry and Milly grinned at him.

"Thank you!" Mum beamed. "Now, I've just seen your mum, Milly, and she tells me she's got ice creams for you. Off you go, outside!"

Jamie, Harry and Milly ran out of the study, down the passageway, through the hall and out into the sunshine.

"We did it!" said Milly.

"Hurray!" shouted Harry, spinning around. "That's the end of the Gnome!"

Jamie slapped both their hands in high fives, but he wasn't so sure. He thought of the other stone statues. If there had been other Gnomes in the past, couldn't there be more in the future?

Harry and Milly began to race down the hill. Milly turned to look back at Jamie. "Come on!" she cried.

Jamie shook himself and ran after them, through the long grass, past the old well, the shattered greenhouse and crumbling walls, all the way down to Milly's cottage.

Her mum was standing by the gate, holding out three ice creams.

"Mmmm," Harry said, slurping at his. It trickled down his chin.

"Come on in," Milly's mum said, opening the gate. "I've just made some lemonade."

Milly followed her into the cottage and Harry smiled at Jamie. "We don't have to worry about anything now," he said. He shrugged off his faithful backpack. "Won't be needing that any more," he said, going inside.

Jamie looked at the backpack lying in the long grass. A spindly spider began to scuttle its way across it.

Jamie knelt and scooped up the creature,

carefully placing it in a flower bed. He picked the backpack up, hooking a strap over one shoulder.

"After all," he murmured, "you can never be too careful."

LOOK OUT
*for the other books
in the series. . .*

SNAKE SHOCK

ED GRAVES

CREEPY CREATURES

SPIDER FRIGHT

ED GRAVES

CREEPY CREATURES

BAT ATTACK

ED GRAVES

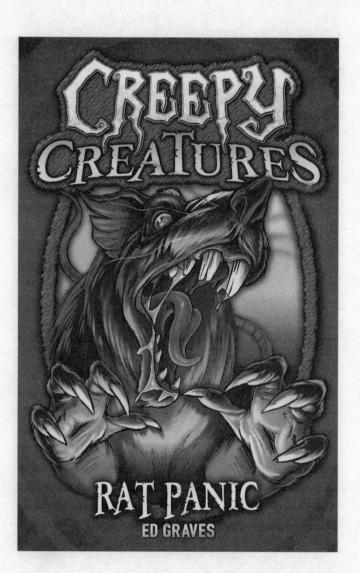

CREEPY CREATURES

RAT PANIC

ED GRAVES